The Incredible Journey of a Neapolitan Puffin

VALERIO GARGIULO

DEDICATION

This book is dedicated to my daughter Aurora, and in memory of my grandmother Giuseppina.

1   Before the Beginning   1

2   The Puffin Dream   13

3   Future is not 'really' mine   22

4   State of Confusion   35

5   Friendship Journey   47

6   The Hidden People   62

7   On the Way   73

8   Winter Solstice   86

9   The Ritual   98

10   Nothing like it seems   106

ACKNOWLEDGMENTS

This book was made possible by the many people who inspired and supported me in numerous ways. I am grateful for the support and guidance provided by my parents, my girlfriend Anna and my aunt Adele. I want to thank also Paolo Gargiulo, Brunella Voto, Cristiano Gargiulo, Alessandro Cernuzzi, Cristina Presti, Joost van Roosmalen, Andree Carmona, Rún Friðriksdóttir, Andre Abud, Dario Farruggia, Vitale Fusco, Jón Viktor and Magnús Már Kristinsson for their feedback and contributions.

I BEFORE THE BEGINNING

My name is Valentino Voto, research assistant, Ph.D. student and cultural adviser at the Neapolitan University of Social Anthropology.

I am a conscientious person who concerns for the welfare of others. The worst part of me was my inability to pick a side because I generally want peace and harmony. From an early age, people remarked that I was courteous, thoughtful and patient.

Anthropology isn't just the study of native cultures, at least not anymore. It's the study of all types of cultures and humans. I knew I wanted to be an anthropologist when I realized that I am interested in human cultures, and their various forms existing in the world.

My doctoral thesis concerned Norse mythology, and paranormal phenomena related to the soothsayers (*spámenn* in Icelandic) and the 'hidden creatures' (*Huldufólk*), the elves in Icelandic folklore.

I played with imaginary friends since childhood. A fanciful child, who loved the idea of a 'buddy' that no one else can see and perceive. Like fictional characters created by a writer: elves, extraterrestrials, and people who did not exist. This got me thinking. I wondered if those kinds of phenomenon were paranormal manifestations or a common psychological and social disorder.

I often doubted the natural order that governs our reality. I was different from other kids, but I felt comfortable with it. I didn't tell anyone except my brother Massimo about my daydreams. He is younger than I. He was diagnosed with autism spectrum disorder when he was three. I never had a problem with that. I looked at him as having a creative brain, which means his brain works differently than mine.

However, he has unique abilities. He could do calculations before any other child in his class. He has an amazing photographic memory and a great knowledge of Greek mythology. Heracles, son of Zeus and strongest man on earth, was his favorite hero. My mom used to call him *ercolino* ('little Hercules') for being also a robust and sturdy child.

Sometimes we played together with these imaginary friends, especially with the alien Titus. I still can clearly describe him. He had a puppet-like face with thin antennas on his head, a small mouth and a huge nose, two arms and two legs like the humans. He was a couple of inches taller than me at that time. His skin was yellowish, and the eyes were like marbles.

I lived for many years in Naples, the third-largest city in Italy. I am proud of my native city. Initially known as Parthenope (the name of one of the Sirens in Greek mythology), it was a settlement established in the second millennium Before Christ.

Many great people, famous worldwide, were born here, such as the most admired Italian operatic tenor Enrico Caruso, and the Academy Award-winner Sophia Loren. Among other things, Neapolitan culture has established its roots in diverse societies throughout the world.

United Nations Educational, Scientific and Cultural Organization (UNESCO) described its Historic Centre as being "of exceptional value", and it added the art of the Neapolitan pizza to the list of "intangible cultural heritage of humanity."

To get a full understanding of my childhood, there is also the fact that Naples was an occult city, where every step follows the relics of the great freemasons and noblemen. The legends and tales, behind the miles of tunnels and catacombs underlying, have constantly stimulated my imagination.

One of the most interesting personalities that inspired me is Raimondo di Sangro, the 'Sorcerer' Prince, more commonly known as Prince of Sansevero.

He was a direct descendant of Charlemagne, King of the Franks and Holy Roman Emperor. Many legends grew up around his memory, but most of all, he was an alchemist.

In one of his more extraordinary experiments, he created a so-called *Palingenesia*, which enabled him to reproduce plants, insects and small animals from their ashes. The origin of the word *Palingenesia* may be traced back to the Stoic philosophers, who used the term for the continual process of re-creation by the Creator (God). Although I would not label myself a Stoic, their ideas apply to our lives even generations later. The universe is still governed by the law of reason. We can't avoid its inexorable force, but we can simply follow the law deliberately.

Another person who inspired me was my high school teacher in ancient Greek culture, Professor Parrella. What I do remember was his human side. I particularly recall the different advice given to me and the other students.

He loved Socrates, a Greek philosopher and the main source of Western thought. He had a favorite sentence from him, which he used to say to us. Here I quote, "True wisdom comes to each of us when we realize how little we understand about life, ourselves, and the world around us."

This quotation means that we cannot teach people anything, as we can only make them think. Learning is a personal experience, and I treasured his lessons in my heart. It's kind of sad that people call philosophy useless when it has so many great values and things we can yet learn.

I lived in an apartment in a large building nearby Sansevero family residence, not far from Santa Chiara, a religious complex that includes a church, a monastery, and tombs. I went to an elementary school within walking distance from my house.

It took ten minutes to get there. Occasionally bullies were waiting for me outside the school gates, and it could have been an adventure to return home safe and sound.

I felt like I was the protagonist of a fantasy novel. I imagined them as an advanced breed of orcs, who have lost faith in mankind. I was scared to death of them, but also fascinated. Through the eyes of a child, raised by loving and protective parents, humble and honest workers, those kids were like savages but in a fantastic view of reality. They were called *scugnizzi*, boys whose only home was the street, where they spent a lot of their lives playing rather than studying or working.

I used the word *zawa-zawa* to describe them, a Japanese onomatopoeia, which sounds much more a fairy tale definition. I had the feeling that someone had stolen their youth.

They were brought into a condition to despair of life, abandoned and left to take care of themselves. Perhaps they were angry with me because I was a happy child. My parents surrounded me with love and affection. I was raised in a stable environment, unlike what they had known.

My parents were immigrants in the North of Italy. My father Antonio started working in 1970 for the state-owned holding company (*Ferrovie dello Stato* in Italian) that manages infrastructure and services on the rail network. They lived at Brenner Pass through the Alps, which forms the border between Italy and Austria.

The Alpine climate becomes colder in winter with lots of snow. My mother Anna never liked to live there. I just think she missed her family, and she had felt particularly isolated and lonely. Then they moved back in 1976 to Naples, which was where my brother and I were born.

I heard lots of ghost tales in Naples during my childhood. I remember one legend that has always fascinated me. A benevolent spirit called *Bella 'mbriana* (meaning 'soul of the house'), a beautiful young woman with a gentle face, invoked to receive advice and divert negative influences.

The folklore tells us about a princess who lost her reason over an unhappy love affair. She wandered the Neapolitan alleys like a lost soul. The father, a king, followed her, rewarding with anonymous gifts those who welcomed and fed the poor daughter.

Thus, was born the tradition of the good fortune associated with her protection of the household. It was in that context that my interest in folktales and superstitious beliefs developed in tandem with the love I feel for anthropology and philosophy.

2 THE PUFFIN DREAM

It was a typical day in Naples. I began to be tired to the *status quo*. The heat produced a drowsy effect. Although it was the end of November, it was still unusually warm.

I was working on an article for my Ph.D. project and I couldn't stop. I realized one thing about a doctorate. It is not for everyone. Sometimes, I felt guilty because of my research's progress, even though I had a huge motivation. I knew I needed to believe in me. I often had extreme anxiety, but at night it was at its worse. I couldn't get it under control. I struggled with it for a while. I was bored and dissatisfied, and I began to search for meaning in my life. I realized that only I can change it for the better.

I understood that if you get a deep feeling of regret and sadness, then this is a good sign that you are not living your highest purpose. I needed to leave my native town for my studies to move forward. Surely that was not the only reason. I desired to be free too.

I was studying to be a professor one day. Not because I wanted to make loads of money, or because I wanted to be someone with high social status or the highest possible level of education. But most of all, I wanted to be able to do something meaningful.

My oneiric activity was intense at that time. Occasionally, I couldn't recall the last few minutes before I fell asleep.

My mind faded into unconsciousness. Unfortunately, I was unable to remember everything in-between. Since then, I took a precaution; a diary next to my bed, where I wrote all the details.

I had this recurring dream about a bird, the *Fratercula arctica,* also known as the Atlantic puffin.

The following description tells what generally took place.

As I got out of the bed everything seemed to be in slow motion. I walked to the front room area. I looked outside through the glass window. I was in a sort of lunar landscape.

When a bright light appeared, a flock of puffins came up, flying towards me. They were so charming that I was in awe of their beauty. They happily allowed me to touch their beautiful feathers. Then I walked inside a barn, and everyone inside looked like a puffin. They were all working hard stacking sacks of food. I stood at the foot of a big desk, and the foot of the desk was taller than me. In that place, there was a young lady with bright blue eyes.

She looked at me and said, "Let's see if I can find your name in this book." The book was large in size and it covered most of the top of the big desk.

There were two other birds sitting on a windowsill. Probably they were ravens. They both shouted my name: "Valentino!" I remember their names. *Pensiero* and *Memoria.* I am impressed by the fact that they talked to me, and that they were sort of enjoying themselves. At that point, I usually woke up.

I didn't want the dream to end, as it made me feel so in peace. I recognized the puffins because they had a black cap head, a face that was mainly white, and orange-red feet. Indeed, puffins are a small species of short-winged and short-tailed seabirds.

The largest population is found in Iceland. *Lundi* is the Icelandic word. I thought the two ravens represented the messengers of what was to come.

The North Germanic peoples took dreams seriously. They viewed them as a sort of flash to the reality of a parallel universe. According to Norse Mythology, puffin represented self-acceptance and self-empowerment.

I found it curious that *Pulcinella di mare* is the Italian word for puffin and also a classical character in Neapolitan puppetry. Indeed, Pulcinella is a traditional dark mask with a hooked, beak-like nose, that originated in 1500.

Inspired by this character, there is also a neoclassical ballet by Russian composer Igor Stravinsky.

The surprising thing is that the story of the mask seems inspired by an Icelandic saga, written in the Thirteenth Century.

As reported by a tradition preserved in the chronicle of Grettir Ásmundarson (a bellicose outlaw), druids wore birds' masks to scare off evil spirits during the course of a ritual. They were Celtic priests, and this was not just a religion. It was a lifestyle.

Definitely, these two traditions merged somehow and had some points in common to me. Even though, it was unclear whether this anecdote was factual or legend.

My idea was that the script could have been brought to Western Europe by Celtic traders through the Alpine region. Records of ritual traditions involving birds' masks can be found throughout ancient history.

Indeed, masks similar to the ones used by druids have been made in Italy since the 2nd century AD.

I have been fascinated with paganism and the occult since I was a kid. We know so little about the world. It seemed to me that the less control over the environment, the higher the belief in supernatural and occult were. Ancient Iceland settlers experienced a wide range of extreme weather and climate events. They were completely and totally at the mercy of the natural environment.

Through the centuries, they have formulated their beliefs to survive and live safely in a difficult world. These types of stories and beliefs encouraged me to go directly there.

I was the protagonist of an adventure that led me out of my geographic and temporal boundaries. I was about to leave for Reykjavik. It was a journey that had taken me over 2,700 miles.

3 FUTURE IS NOT 'REALLY' MINE

In the weeks leading up to my trip, I began to build my network of contacts in Iceland. I was going through the biggest change in my life. I had an Ecuadorian friend living in Reykjavik, his name Felix Ortega.

We met on an American cruise ship, where we both worked as entertainers. When I joined the ship at the age of nineteen, I was amazed at how quickly connections and friendships were formed. Felix became my best mate. He was an adventurer, a lover of the mountains, and extreme sports. He wanted at all costs to host me for the first weeks in Iceland.

He called me a short time later after receiving my email. "Hello bro', when are you coming? I cannot wait to see you again," he said with his unmistakable Latin American accent. He loved Italy, and I remember he frequently asked me to help him with my native language on the ship. Although he had sometimes confused a few words, he spoke good Italian.

"My dear Felix, I'll arrive next Saturday," I replied, pleased to have a companion waiting for me in that distant land. We said goodbye, both excited and happy to spend time together again.

Besides Felix, I could also count on Jón and Fanney. Professor Jón Magnússon would have been my thesis supervisor. He was a professor of cultural anthropology at the Universities of Iceland and Cologne; as well as an expert in runes, the old alphabet used by the ancient Germanic peoples. Jón was married to Fanney Pállsdóttir. She was the teacher and director of the Academy of Seltjarnarnes, a school where it was possible to learn about Icelandic folklore, such as elves, gnomes, trolls and mountain spirits. In any case, everything was ready.

I made a video call to announce my arrival.

"Good morning, thank you for your availability. I would like to inform you that next week I will finally be in Iceland," I said firmly and professionally.

"Very good Valentino, what a pleasure. I am sure you will be comfortable here with us," Jón replied solemnly.

He gave me some information about registration at the university, "Probably, the staff of the secretary's office of the Ph.D. program might not have time to explain everything regarding the contract in detail. However, it will be signed for one semester at a time, and you will be offered a new contract for the upcoming semester."

"Thank you again, for everything. It sounds like a great plan," I responded, feeling honored and delighted.

After the video call terminated, I found myself surrounded by a quiet and peaceful atmosphere. I was enthusiastic. Years ago, my life was so static. I thought that nothing was worth it anymore. And then I started this doctoral program. Having this early conversation with my tutor made my day, and I could finally focus my attention on the next project.

My interest in mystery led me to refine and extend my studies of Norse mythology and paranormal phenomena. Jón sent me some interesting material that provided my research with new topics to be explored.

I started reading some articles about pagan beliefs and Christianity. I got into runes seemingly out of nowhere, and I found some interesting insights.

Runestones were used by Norsemen during the Viking Age as tools of divination to predict the future. I learned a few different things that surprised me. There were several instances of divination in the Bible used in both the Old and New Testament in the form of 'casting lots'.

The word divination means literally 'to be inspired by a god', and it's the practice of discovering information about current and future events by interpreting omens or supernatural signs.

Since the Christianization of the Anglo-Saxon Kingdoms in the AD 597, priests would cast runes to determine the will of God. Prophets were technically diviners. They determined the destiny connecting to the Almighty through prayer and ritual. Even the act of worship itself, in any religion or belief, was a form of divination. It was everywhere, permeated into the most basic of religious practices.

I realized that parts of what is known, it was rewritten by Christian settlers to fit the general theme of good against evil. Their purpose was to increase conversion of the Viking population to their religion. For example, *Jötunn* (a type of entity in Norse mythology, presumably a sort of giant) was never malevolent, but a force of nature and magical power.

The word was ambiguously defined. Therefore, *Jötunn* had his positive and negative sides, but there was a supernaturally determined balance between them.

To be effective, the recognition of evil required a prior establishment of a system of ethics. It seemed like a relative rather than an absolute concept, which made me think harder. A lack of ethics allowed one to ignore the consequence of sin.

Ignoring evil was step one to wander off to commit it. Knowledge of ethics, the absolute standard for how to act and not act, was a great chance to avoid an offense. Once ethics were acknowledged, Christians could practice them.

In my view, the very concept of 'malignity' was kind of slippery. Evil was just a fancy word for 'stuff we don't like', and it was a pretty subjective thing.

Earthquakes seem nefarious to Pompeii residents, but on the other hand, geological activities made the Earth viable for human life to begin with.

The perception of evil became like a very real thing in a metaphysical sense. We can't stand an evil person, but we could do a harmful act towards others in most cases of self-defense.

For instance, a gun makes police officers' jobs easier, but it can also be used in terrorist attacks to threaten a person or kill. It depends upon the intentions.

There are so many cases and different dynamics. Bad decisions teach wrong behaviors, but good decisions instead are taken through positive experiences.

Since the puffin's dreams occurred, the notebook was a useful tool for collecting memory traces. I loved writing things down, as it was also a way to express myself. I had a dream once about an old neighbor: Mrs. Esposito was going to pass away from breast cancer. What I find hard to believe is that a week later it just happened.

There was no way for me to know that this lady was already sick. Only a predetermined future could give me that sight because it seemed impossible by laws of physics or biology for me to have a premonition of the upcoming event.

Well, if that was the case, the future is not 'really' mine. A premonition is a feeling with no connection to rational thinking. It is different from a prophecy, the way in which God at times spoke to prophets, giving them a specific message to share with other people. It's hard to accept that everything could be predetermined.

The ancient Greeks believed that the Gods were in charge of everything affecting human life. Life was considered like a stage, where we are playing a role and wearing masks. In this personification, everything was predetermined for them.

I come from a Catholic family, so I went to church every Sunday. Maybe the 'Creator' made us responsible for our actions within a frame.

Perhaps prayers helped me to please God to forgive my sins. My grandmother Giuseppina prayed for me and my siblings until the last hours she was alive. She passed away a few years ago.

Giuseppina was my rock, the one I could always confide in. She survived World War II. She resided in downtown Naples in a big apartment at the market street of *Pignasecca*.

She was a seamstress. After World War II, NATO base installations were located in Bagnoli, a western seaside quarter area. She used to make uniforms to be used by American soldiers.

Giuseppina had a sister called Anna who was a tailor as well. Her friends called her Ninella, and she adopted the nickname. She was 12 years old and contracted bacterial meningitis.

Despite the handicap, she was able to lead a normal life. The two sisters lived together until Ninella's death. She died in the early 90s.

My grandfather Salvatore was a stubborn man. He had a hard life. I do not doubt that. He lived his entire childhood at the orphanage. Because of his Second World War service, he received the Italian War Merit Cross (in Italian: *Croce al Merito di Guerra*).

He worked as a gardener at the municipal parks and gardens. He died when I was about five years of age. Unfortunately, I was very young, so I don't remember much of him. This makes me sad. I would have liked to spend more time with him.

4 STATE OF CONFUSION

I am not ashamed to admit that ghost stories have always fascinated me. I have always been interested in paranormal activities since I was 15 years old.

The existence of them have been debated for centuries. The questions of why some can and yet others cannot see or sense the presence of these entities has been contested with numerous theories.

My mother Anna had such experiences. This was the scariest event she remembered. She told me the following spooky story.

When she was a young girl, her parents rented an old apartment in *Concezione a Montecalvario* street. The building was attached to an old Baroque monastery. The flat was big and full of antique furniture. The couple before them had moved out when their two months old baby died. She experienced some scary phenomena that occurred there.

Three weeks after moving in, my mother woke up in the middle of the night to the sound of a baby crying. She felt distinctly uncomfortable in that room. But that was only the beginning.

One day she decided to explore the attic with her sister Simona. They went upstairs to look. The attic was very dusty. In an old dresser, my aunt found one drawer filled with family photographs. In a framed photo, a little girl was pictured on a pony being led by a dwarf dressed as a clown. In another portrait, six men were having a meal on a terrace.

On the wall above a piece of furniture, three paintings showing a sad figure, a girl swinging on a hammock tied to a tree, and ballerina shoes on tiptoes. A child probably made them.

In the next drawer, there were many rosaries of many shapes and sizes. The Holy Rosary is a form of prayer used in the Catholic Church and a devotion dedicated to the Virgin Mary. They were very beautiful works of art.

The day after my mother heard loud noises from upstairs as if the furniture were moved around. All night long she sensed something tapping on the roof and against the windows. During these noises, the rosaries began appearing all over her room: in a drawer, or inside a closet. When my mother put them back, all the rosaries moved magically to a different drawer. When a priest came and blessed the apartment, all of the paranormal activity stopped.

It is not strange if this story has been forever in my memory. It was creepy.

All types of bizarre circumstances occurred at this house. Nevertheless, I assumed that something inexplicable happened. I know my mother Anna. She is very talkative. Although she liked to exaggerate stories, she always had a great accuracy to recall these events.

I don't know for sure about the existence of paranormal events. Certainly, I have great respect for the supernatural world and the 'unseen'. I realized that one should not be playing around with something unexplainable and without a certain awareness and knowledge.

The day before my trip to Iceland, I had a strange and inexplicable experience. I was late for my last lecture. Then quite unexpectedly, I was surprised by a young lady. I thought maybe she was a tourist asking for directions.

I was walking towards *Spaccanapoli* (literally 'split Naples'), a long road, called in Latin *Decumanus Maximus*. It is a straight and narrow main street of the ancient center of the original Greco-Roman city of Neapolis. Designed in the Greek era, it crosses the downtown in its entirety.

Her eyes were magnetic, of a gray-green color. She looked like a familiar face, though I was sure I did not know her. She touched my soul the first time I saw her. She arrived from San Domenico Maggiore, one of the most important squares. She approached me, and I was surprised by her elegant ways to speak.

"Hello Valentino, I am Gudrun," she said in a perfect Italian accent. She was incredibly beautiful. She wore vintage jeans and a sweater that had bizarre and geometric designs.

"Hi, do we know each other?" I answered still confused. She appeared alarmed, and said, "We have to do it soon. Remember the manuscript?"

Then she started to tell me how the members of a sect of intellectuals, philosophers and bankers would have the ability to contact the hidden creatures to obtain earthly benefits.

"They will be trying to perform the ritual again. They are evil. They are greedy. They are the Sorcerers of Hólmavík!"

I didn't know what to believe at that point.

"*Draumfarir tíðar, mun hurðum upp ljúka,*" she repeated this sentence two or three times, before vanishing into thin air. Suddenly I realized that the girl who had stopped me had volatilized. I immediately thought it was a sort of hallucination.

Maybe my mind was playing tricks on me. On the other hand, it seems that 'Déjà vu' is caused precisely by an abnormality of the brain. It was not the first time that happened to me, but it was so real.

I was struck by that phrase: *Draumfarir tíðar, mun hurðum upp ljúka.* I reached into my pocket and I realized that there was a piece of paper with that sentence on it. Apparently, she also signed her name on it: Gudrun Oddsdóttir. An Icelandic name for sure!

This was most definitely not a figment of my imagination. Did she leave this text for me? What was she talking about? A sect? A ritual? Was that weird experience related to my upcoming trip?

Maybe this episode had nothing to do with it. Perhaps, this could be the answer to the dreams I've been having about ravens and puffins?

When I went back home, I started doing some research. Unfortunately, the internet did not help much. I searched a little more thoroughly and finally found something. 'Vivid dreams will eventually open gates', this was the meaning.

The same sentence was on a Sixteenth-Century manuscript, translated into English by professor Jón himself. An obscure ancient medieval grimoire. A textbook of magic, which contained a collection of rituals, spells, and staves. This document included also legends, myths, and folktales.

Close to the enigmatic sentence, it was shown the image of the bound Fenrir. The ancient Fenrir's cult was the religious practice of the worshiping of wolfs among the Norseman. He was the God of all gods.

All gods were fearful of him. In fact, he represented a creature that was dangerous, hungry and cunning at the same time. A big evil wolf, seen as a symbol of chaos.

I was taught in high school by Professor Parrella that manuscripts of those types contain at most a kernel of truth. Nevertheless, they were very sought after by rich people in the past. Therefore, it was well known that scam artists would create books of weird pics and gibberish, just to try to sell them at amazing amounts of money.

It appears that the text's alphabet was a bunch of mysterious letters made from a dream. Usually, grimoires need to be decrypted. They weren't meant to be read by anyone other than the writer. They were personal, supposed to remain private to the practitioner who built them.

I decided to deepen this manuscript from a scientific point of view. The chapter in question confirmed what the mysterious Gudrun told me. That sentence would be part of an epitaph written on a grave. I also learned that the *Sorcerers of Hólmavík* existed historically.

There was a medieval priest, Berengario di Altavilla, that reported an episode in which members of this sect would gather around a tomb in Skagaströnd every year in the Icelandic region of Norðurland. According to his testimony, they were performing a ritual in old Norse to obtain from Fenrir further powers of knowledge, wisdom and even intervention in the material world. They used knowledge of the occults to influence the world.

Who was that girl? How could she just vanish like that? Was she the girl of my dreams or a ghost? I don't know if this was possible, but I fell in love with her. Yes, I was in love with this girl. How could an unknown person have this effect on me?

Well, I don't know if she was a real person or just my imagination. In doubt, I trusted that all possibilities may be considered. I told myself it was better to have faith. That's why my journey started with great expectations.

5 FRIENDSHIP JOURNEY

The big day had finally come. "Valentino, get ready, then I'll take you to the airport," my father said. My mother kept telling me to just take care of myself and be careful.

She told me that she would pray to Gerard Majella, a saint by the Catholic Church. His intercession was often sought for children. To her, I and my brother were still her little boys.

Massimo also accompanied me. He was rather taciturn. Maybe he knew it was a risk, or maybe he missed me already. He looked up at me, silent for a moment, and said, "Titus will protect you, he will keep you from harm!" Sometimes his way of speaking would, therefore, seem to be enigmatic, as if he wanted to warn me.

When we got there, my father told me to always wear a woolen shirt to protect myself from cold and moisture. I laughed because the advice was so typical of him, constantly worried that someone he loves will get sick.

"I will take care, and when I arrive I will call you." I do hate long goodbyes. I turned my back and headed towards the terminal.

The flight had a stopover in Frankfurt before it continued to Iceland. On the plane, I met an Italian guy, Carlo Cacciatori. We immediately became friends.

He stood close to me. His family immigrated to Germany in search of better opportunities. Once he started talking, he never stopped until landing. In three hours and a half, we discussed several different topics.

"I am a mechanical engineer. And I also work for a nonprofit organization that helps teenagers in need. Sometimes I teach them how to fix cars, or how to make pizza dough," he said proudly.

Carlo had his own style of talking. He reminded me a lot of Al Pacino's character from 'Scent of a Woman', which was a remake of an Italian film, *Profumo di donna*. He was a charming and sophisticated man. I told him I was leaving Naples for Reykjavik.

"Are you prepared to spend the next couple of months in snowstorms, dark nights, wind and cold?" he said sarcastically. "I am sure I will be able to adapt," I replied smiling.

I remember that we had a conversation about discrimination and exclusion by being a foreigner within another cultural context.

"Many immigrant groups are like puppets of an unpredictable chain of events," he said. Carlo was concerned about that, but he admitted how lucky he was.

"My family came from Italy in the 1970s. They abandoned all their possessions and left. My mother always told me that Germany was a place of hope for those who desired to get a better future."

I thought, listening to him, that if God exists and he saw this disturbing trend in many areas of our world in the direction of intolerance and racism, he was probably angry and ashamed of us.

Another topic was the debate between free will and destiny. "I don't think we are all born with the same chance. The circumstances in which we find ourselves in every day are probably matters of fate," he sadly admitted.

In his view, we have little control over most things; whatever happens, we should accept any circumstances and leave them as they come.

I felt that I and Carlo had similar values and a common understanding of how the world works. We kept talking until we landed. When we were out of the plane, we walked together until Terminal I of Frankfurt Airport.

"I have to go. I need to catch my connecting flight," I stated, and Carlo gave me a big hug before saying goodbye. I had enjoyed his company. I certainly met a good friend. I had a few more minutes there, then it was time for me to board the next aircraft.

6.30 pm, Keflavik International Airport. Finally, in Iceland, land of lava and ice, lunar landscapes and Old Norse mythology; but also, of a recent financial crisis.

In this regard, Jón's manuscript came to my mind. So, I thought to myself: does the sect still exist today? Was the 2008 financial crisis caused by the Sorcerers of Hólmavík? What was their purpose? Why did the sect choose Iceland? How did they pull strings behind the scenes?

I was spiraling a little bit. So many questions were unanswered. Probably I was just a tired and overexcited traveler. However, I was continuing to make strange conjectures and suppositions. I imagined a world of corrupt and powerful men, dedicated to anything mysterious and disquieting to gain economic power and influence.

An Enlightenment-era secret society, in which their affiliates were free to control world affairs, and there was no way to know their plots. An elite of persons who have acquired great financial, political and religious influence over the centuries.

They were probably men of wide knowledge, connoisseurs of culture and social structures, which gave them the ability to manipulate a nation's beliefs and behaviors.

Fortunately, I reached my destination. My mind has often generated various kinds of irrational thoughts, mostly based on a fervid imagination, and it was not the first time I engaged in such flights of fancy.

When I went outside the airport doors, Felix was already there waiting for me with open arms. "*Hola* Valentino, welcome to Iceland!" he said enthusiastically.

He was wearing black cargo pants with large side pockets. A pair of yellow sneakers with blue and red sections: the colors of the Ecuadorian flag, I thought. He worked as a mountain guide. Trained at the highest level, he had many years of climbing experience.

Felix spent his entire adolescence exploring the remote Andes mountains, accompanying his father for scientific explorations. Don Pablo Ortega was a speleologist and physicist at the University of Quito.

Amongst other things, Don Pablo organized the first guided tours along the north side of the Cordillera del Condor, a mountain range between Ecuador and Peru.

"Thank you very much, Felix, for picking me up!" I said. Therefore, as ancient Greek philosopher Epicurus said, "Of all the means to ensure happiness throughout the whole life, by far the most important is the acquisition of friends."

We were happy as we hugged each other and somehow made it into his car. Anyway, five years passed since we worked together on a cruise ship. There were so many things to say, and we had so many stories to tell. It was a long journey between the airport and the center of Reykjavik. We had enough time to catch up a little bit.

Even though it was winter it was not that cold outside. However, climate variability and weather extremes affect this small island nation, such as the alternation of light and dark periods. I was immediately struck by the vastness of the lava desert and its intense colors.

Icelandic glaciers are huge sheets of moving ice that can be seen from a considerable distance.

That place touched my soul. This type of climate is unstable, characterized by a large daily and annual temperature range. The Icelandic winter is known for being cold and dark. I kept thinking about how to cope with three or four months of darkness. I was trying to figure it out until my thoughts were interrupted by Felix.

"And you still haven't told me why you came to Iceland for your thesis," he asked curiously.

"I'm interested in local legends, and I'm looking for someone who had an encounter with elves," I said.

Felix burst into a roar of laughter. "Who are you now a paranormal investigator?" he ironically commented.

However, he was not unfamiliar with supernatural and inexplicable events. He was raised in a family where transcendence was instilled into his mind. His father also had a passion to work with pastors and churches across Quito. Don Pablo, moreover, firmly believed in the existence of intelligent extraterrestrial life.

"How long will you stay in Iceland?" he asked. "I'm not sure," I hesitated before answering, momentarily lost looking at a map, "It depends on how everything is going at the end of the next summer."

I was trying to find the precise location of Skagaströnd. It was far away from Reykjavik at glance.

"I would like to visit the north coast of Iceland. I will do some research there, and then I will make some inquiries about local history. Would you like to accompany me?" I asked. "Yes, of course, I have some free time next weekend," he replied.

Felix had an old 1983 GMC Vandura van. It was the same model used in the American television series A-Team. He bought the vehicle from an Icelandic man who had been employed at the NATO base. The US military left Iceland in fall 2006. The base was built during World War II, and then later it became a Cold War outpost to monitor the movements of the former Soviet Union.

"In my spare time, I customized the van with the sole purpose of always being ready for a new adventure. Now I can drive everywhere, even the most remote areas of the island," he told me with a certain pride.

After a long drive, the van stopped. We arrived at Felix's house in *Suðurgata*, a street located just west of downtown Reykjavik. We got in and climbed up to the second floor. It was a small but cozy apartment.

"I've been living here for 5 years and I feel very comfortable; it's quiet most of the time and my neighbors are friendly," he explained.

We spent a relaxing rest of the evening. Felix uncorked a bottle of red wine for the occasion, and I poured us each a glass.

We both loved pasta dishes, so I decided to cook for us a spicy *spaghetti aglio e olio* (with garlic and olive oil), an easy and quick Neapolitan recipe.

We kept talking until I realize how late it was. So, I decided to go to sleep. "I'll go to bed. I need some rest," I said, wishing Felix goodnight. I had to get up early the next day to meet Jón and Fanney. I was exhausted but happy.

6 THE HIDDEN PEOPLE

The alarm clock sounded. I woke up in an instant, surrounded by darkness. The blinds were tightly closed. It was a few hours before the meeting.

I had enough time to prepare myself for the day ahead. I stayed in bed a few more minutes thinking about Gudrun. I thought also about Jón and Fanney.

I wanted to make a good impression. I had spent some time wondering just what I would say to them and what they might think of me. I convinced myself that fate brought me in Iceland, and I decided to not worry at all. After that, I was finally up, and I started to get ready for the day.

Felix was still sleeping. I decided not to wake him up so early. Even though he moved abroad by his own choice, he missed his family and felt homesick.

The kitchen was full of pictures of days gone by: his parents and grandparents, sister and brother, photos of him in the act of climbing, the Snæfellsjökull glacier, and his excursion into its depths. Felix loved to dwell in memories. After an abundant breakfast, I walked out.

It was a wet and dark morning. My initial impression of the neighborhood was that it was a rather bleak looking place. There was a kind of claustrophobic feeling outside. Despite this discomfort, I felt also a strange sensation of peace.

The apartment was a stone's throw away from the old Hólavallagarður cemetery. The name means 'garden on a hill'. Only few trees were planted in the graveyard. Iceland was once heavily forested, but deforestation and consequent erosion occurred so quickly.

The wife of a magistrate was the first person buried there. According to a popular legend, she became also a sort of graveyard's guardian, who would watch over the tombs for all time.

The university was not far. Indeed, it was just a walk across the street from Suðurgata, so I didn't have to worry about being late.

I continued walking south a few minutes, until I came to a route for pedestrians and cyclists. I arrived at the University of Iceland. I was told by Jón to go directly to the office block closest to the entrance. The Institute for Social and Cultural Anthropology was not difficult to find.

A door just opened, and the professor was standing there waiting for me. Jón was a huge man of middle age with broad shoulders.

He reminded me of *Mangiafuoco* ('Fire eater'), the fictional puppet master from the popular children's novel Pinocchio. He had a big black beard exactly like him, which I thought was sort of unusual for an Icelander.

However, his personality did not fit his size. He impressed me immediately with his cordial mood. "Hey Valentino, please come in," his voice was calm and kind. Fanney moved next to him, grabbed my hands, and said friendly, "I am very pleased to meet you. I know you were looking forward to be here."

"Thank you Fanney. I am very pleased to meet you as well. Yes, I was really excited about this upcoming project," I answered with a smile.

She was an elegant lady with light brown hair and blue eyes. Jón brought me a chair. Then he poured me a cup of American coffee.

Besides his work on the old Norse literature, Jón also wrote books on Icelandic folktales and legends. As reported by his recent survey, a high percentage of Icelanders believed in the existence of elves and ghosts.

"There are Icelanders who live in direct contact with the land, the sea and the wild nature. This will seem strange to you, but there are many here who believe in the presence of a variety of invisible person-like entities," Jón admitted, but he had another opinion about it.

"I have never personally seen elves or other hidden creatures, and I have never met a ghost; but I must admit I've heard a lot of stories," he said.

Unlike the Irish fairytale tradition, and the Germanic mythology, the Huldufólk were similar to human beings, sharing their appearance and behavior.

There was, for instance, a curious episode involving road construction crews. The local government was almost forced to contact a medium, because equipment continuously broke and working tools were lost.

The project for a new road involved the destruction of a large rock, known as *Álfhóll* and meaning 'Elfhill'. According to the psychic, that hill was the home of some elves. The digger broke every time they approached that big rock. The trucks used were found repeatedly overturned.

In the end, a compromise was found acceptable to its 'inhabitants'. The rock was carefully transported to another place.

This type of belief in elves and other creatures no longer exists in the Western world because of the great monotheistic religions. Christianity had therefore always been predominated in Europe and had left no room for previous pagan cults. In the Middle Ages, however, Icelanders adapted to the Church, but at the same time, they continued to pass on the legends about the 'hidden people', since the Vikings first landed on the island.

Fanney pointed out that this isolation from the rest of the world allowed the soul to remain pure from the spiritual contaminations of modern society, which is now too technological and materialistic.

"I have my own idea about it," she said.

"Some Icelanders have preserved their ability to see beyond physical reality. Just as blind and deaf-mutes, who have a sense of taste and smell more developed than others, our people have retained a sensory possibility of communicating, listening and interacting with those creatures."

Maybe the secret of Iceland lies in its nature, which is like an enigma or a code to be deciphered. The earth is still in formation here, due to the intense activity that takes place in its subsoil.

Perhaps in the past, the population has begun to turn to the supernatural, finding no explanation for the natural phenomena to which the island is constantly subjected.

When I started studying occultism, it seemed unlikely that this great spread of irrational ideas could only be the fruit of superstitions and popular ignorance. I always thought there was something bigger. I was fascinated by these stories. Even in Italy, despite the Catholicism, many local cults and popular traditions survived. I know it sounds weird, but still today spells and liturgical dances are celebrated around a fire.

The conversation we had was very interesting. It was that kind of meeting that really inspires you and I felt so blessed and lucky to have met them.

"May we continue next week?" Jón said. He was going abroad for few days, invited as a speaker at an international conference on interpretive anthropology, metaphysics, and paranormal in Madrid.

"Sure. Meantime I will go off on an excursion along the north coast of Iceland and do some research in Skagaströnd," I replied. I looked up at him and he had a worried look on his face. "Be careful Valentino! Weather is often unpredictable in Iceland. You could easily get stuck somewhere."

I reassured him that I planned to go there with my friend Felix, an expert mountain guide. Fanney smiled, as she opened the door for me. "Well, all right, then. See you next week!" "Very well, thank you for this meeting," and I left the office.

7 ON THE WAY

We left early the next morning for Skagaströnd. It was located some 165 miles away from Reykjavik. It was dark outside, and gradually the city disappeared behind us.

I made a *frittata di maccheroni* with leftovers, a fried pasta dish typical of the Neapolitan tradition. An ideal portable travel meal. Felix overhauled his old truck and filled up gasoline and oil.

It was time to reveal the details of my mission to him. I wanted to be honest with Felix. After all, I just needed to collect clues and evidence for my studies. Also, I wished to find out more about my beautiful Gudrun. Nevertheless, I did not know what could happen to us.

Was it dangerous up there? Probably yes. How wicked were these people? I thought they were probably the world's most evil. What type of ritual did the sect perform? Perhaps a ritual to unbound Fenrir in order to gain some mysterious power from him.

What was the link between Gudrun and me? It could be something that had to do with my dreams and premonitions. What was I truly searching for? Looking for Gudrun, or finding myself? I couldn't answer yet those questions.

According to the manuscript, the Sorcerers of Hólmavík had a meeting every year at the cemetery of Skagaströnd. The ritual occurred previously on the longest night during the winter solstice.

"Felix I must tell you that we are going to spy on the ritual of a dangerous sect," I said bluntly. "Are you kidding Valentino?" He answered and began to laugh out loud. "I'm not joking, it's about powerful and unscrupulous people, but I aim to understand if they exist," I admitted.

"So, it's not true that you want to ask simple questions to fishermen about elves and fairy tales for children?" He asked, eyeing me ironically. "No, but I promise you Felix," I reassured him, "We will not take stupid risks."

He had no problem with my crazy story, which rather aroused his curiosity. He took the opportunity to share with me his personal supernatural experience.

When he was 12 years old, he had an encounter with a malevolent entity. He was on vacation with his father in Urbina, a small village located in the central Ecuadorian Andes. Their summer house was a stop-over for the old Guayaquil & Quito Railway. Near this area was the road leading to the Chimborazo volcano, the highest mountain in Ecuador.

It was a beautiful villa with an apartment upstairs and downstairs. According to the local townspeople, many bad things happened before his father bought it.

A native architect was hired by the government to build the house. However, this man suffered from depression and, one day, threw himself off the balcony.

By 1936 the railway was completed, and the house stood empty for years afterward. In the 1970s, Ortega's family bought it and used it for their vacations. They experienced inexplicable phenomena since their first time there. For example, cups and glasses crashed suddenly to the floor, and lights randomly turned on and off.

In the middle of a foggy night, Felix heard loud lamentations from upstairs. As he walked up to the stairs, he saw a ghostly figure standing on the corridor. The spirit pointed his finger at Felix and told him to be quiet. Scared to death, he ran into his father's room. Don Pablo searched the villa everywhere, but he found nothing except an open window leading onto a balcony.

"Believe me, Valentino, it was a horrible experience. I will always remember it," he stated, interrupting his story. He was aware that anything is possible on earth, even the existence of such a sect.

Unexpectedly, I looked at the sky and then I saw with my own eyes a beautiful *aurora borealis.* "Watch the northern lights!" I said to Felix, admiring a wonderful spectacle.

Continuing with his ghost story, he did not pay any attention to me. But then he stopped and replied, "You know, to me it's a bit like in New York, where people who live there no longer notice how tall can be a skyscraper."

"Yes, very funny!" I exclaimed. "But this is my first time and it is amazing." It appeared as a mix of colored lights and sparkles. All so impressive. I felt as I was sucked into another dimension, where space and time were a single entity.

We drove on Highway One toward Skagaströnd. Four hours later we arrived at our guest house, named 'Ferdamadur Inn'. *Ferðamaður* is an Icelandic word which means 'tourist', 'traveler'.

Erna, the innkeeper, was waiting for us. She was a wide-faced young lady with bright blue eyes. She was not particularly friendly, but not rude. I thought maybe she was just shy.

Her voice was soft as she whispered. "Welcome to Skagaströnd, this is the key to the room. Breakfast is served from 6:30 in the lounge." We were tired from the long drive. After we ate something, then we went to bed.

Unfortunately, I could not sleep. I felt a sensation of panic and anguish. Suddenly I heard a sound from a distance, but at first, I could not understand what it was. It sounded like a child singing, exactly like in horror movies. Somehow, I was afraid to open my eyes. I was terrified. I was sweating cold. I felt my heart beating faster through my chest.

I did not want to wake Felix up, but I was almost tempted to do it. Someone called my name. It seemed all true. "Valentino, Valentino!" However, I wanted to convince myself that I was simply tired. Maybe it was another 'trick' of my imagination or at least the sound of the wind. In any case, I was confused, and I could not calm myself down. Somehow the night passed.

The next morning, I went early downstairs for breakfast. I was alone. Felix was still getting ready. Erna was drinking a cup of coffee. I did not know if it was the right time to talk with her. I was still frightened, and I did not pay attention to form and time. So, I told her about my awful night.

Her reaction surprised me because she was not at all surprised. She immediately pointed out that perceiving these voices was a good omen, especially for a stranger.

It meant I was welcome!

"I had my own experience with an elf as a child. I also saw ghosts and dead people, but these entities have never been hostile to me. On the contrary, they are indifferent to my presence," she admitted, "For me they are real."

I asked her if she could say more about the 'hidden people'. "Yes, of course, but I hope you will not have a strange idea about me," she responded as if she was afraid of not being believed. I reassured her she did not have to worry about anything. "Respect is essential when it comes to personal experiences," I said with conviction.

"I have no prejudices. I am a researcher and I usually apply the scientific method, but I am aware of the existence of phenomena that cannot be explained by our traditional approach," I remarked. "Alright then," she nodded. I had my tablet ready to record her story. And with that, she began to tell me about this episode.

"I was nine years old and I was in Siglufjörður, my hometown. One day I was playing alone and jumping from a big rock. When I fell to the ground, a strange creature appeared before me. It was very funny.

He looked like a dwarf. He was normally proportionated, but not taller than a six-year-old child.

He told me it was a beautiful day, but he could not leave his house. He greeted me and gave me a torc[1].

The story reminded me of my childhood. After all, even myself as a kid, I had my supernatural experiences with aliens and other fantastic creatures. Maybe it was simply a fervid imagination. Perhaps even Erna was a bored child, who played with imaginary friends.

"Do you still have that neck-ring?" I asked. "Yes, of course, I always carry it with me," she replied with a big smile, "It's my protective talisman from the evil spirits of the night." She proudly showed me.

It was so tiny that I could not even see it.

---

[1] In Viking age, a torc was a neckless, made generally in silver.

"Although this neckless is proof that I was not dreaming that day, I have never tried to convince anyone. I just keep away from the skeptics," she said firmly.

Felix came. He had a quick breakfast. He was ready to flush out the Sorcerers of Hólmavík. Before letting me go with him, Erna explained that humans cannot see elves and other hidden creatures unless they want to meet us. Therefore, only those with a pure heart could see them.

8 WINTER SOLSTICE

I asked myself: did I seriously believe that Erna met an elf during her childhood? Yes, I did. And, what's more, I was totally impressed by the fact that she trusted me as well. Of course, I found her story to have a striking resemblance to my creation of imaginary friends.

Even though, I began more and more to see from a better perspective what modern humans simply regard as superstition or pagan beliefs.

I think we should learn from old Norse traditions. The 'truth' could more easily exist in these contexts than in our predetermined vision. Part of the problem is that this 'truth' cannot be taught. It could be realized or experienced.

Sadly, we lost connection with 'Mother Earth', which seems to protect and hide from humans some kind of invisible world. How would humanity react if elves or other hidden creatures really exist?

Iceland's pristine nature could be considered as the last bulwark for the preservation and survival of a parallel world, which is invisible to most of us ordinary mortals.

Perhaps, the elves exist only in the mind of suggestible people? Or do they even exist in the real world?

I preferred not telling Felix what happened the night before. I wondered if he would have believed me. Sincerely, I was not even sure if anything really took place at Ferdamadur Inn.

I was probably affected by what was happening around me: my first meeting with Gudrun; the possible existence of a powerful sect; my ongoing thesis work on Norse mythology and paranormal activities; and a mystic journey to Iceland.

We walked along the main street of Skagaströnd. This town was a trading center since the late 15th century. It is now a fishing village. It's a picturesque spot. I loved the tranquility of its coastal area.

It was the day of the winter solstice in the Northern Hemisphere. The shortest day of the year. It always occurs on a specific day: on December 21. It always occurs at a specific time of day: at 11:28 a.m.

In Norse mythology, it was seen as a time of death and rebirth. There were beliefs about the presence of dark spirits descending to Earth during this astronomical phenomenon. Norsemen feared this date. They used to spend most of the midwinter night in the company of one another, to avoid encounters with malevolent entities.

After searching the town through and through, I realized there was no trace of the Sorcerers of Hólmavík, except a beautiful landscape to tourists. We noted nothing suspicious to justify their presence in Skagaströnd.

So, we went to the local cemetery, but again no clues or evidence of an upcoming ritual.

A middle-aged woman, standing in front of an unfinished tomb, attracted my attention. Felix was far behind me. At a certain point, I was not seeing him anymore. The Icelandic lady walked toward me. She greeted me politely. It seemed as if she was waiting for me. She told me that Italy was a country she always wanted to visit.

I don't know how she did it, but somehow, she knew who I was. I didn't need to introduce myself. Her name was Thordis. She had long white hair that she kept in braids, wrapped around her head like a crown. Her skin was very white. She looked deep into my eyes, claiming to possess the gift of foresight.

"I inherited my clairvoyant abilities from my mother. She inherited from my grandmother. My grandmother inherited from my great grandmother. It's been passed down from one generation to another," explained Thordis. She began to analyze my past, present and future without a previous agreement for such purpose.

Putting my two palms together, she traced lines with her fingertip. This was a surprising feeling because I didn't understand what was going on. What she said of my life was pretty interesting: 'I am a person that inspires others to be the best they can be'.

Right after that, she spoke to me again and said something alarming, "I'm sorry you didn't come to me before. Then I would have warned you not to investigate the unknown."

I could hardly believe that she was aware of what I was looking for. Were all these unusual episodes already predestined beforehand?

She pointed her finger to a particular tomb shrine. She said that its structure was aligned precisely to allow the rays of the winter solstice to fall directly on a large stone, which supposed to be the entrance to an elf cave. However, the bad weather often made it impossible to see this magic gate.

Everything became so surreal when these phenomena actually manifested. The sun was almost over the Tropic of Capricorn. The sun's rays began to slant until they pointed directly at the middle of a flat rock. I looked down and saw an entire text engraved on it.

The words were so small as to be almost illegible. I was particularly struck by bird masks painted on the surfaces. They reminded me of those masks used by the druids to keep evil spirits away.

Surprisingly, I recognized the same Gudrun phrase: 'Vivid dreams will eventually open gates'. A few centimeters close to the other figures, there was another familiar scene comprising the bound Fenrir and the sun setting behind a mountain.

Thordis was observing me with an enigmatic look on her face. Talking with her was an intense and tiring experience. I felt like my soul was negatively affected in some way.

Felix finally found me. I was so caught up in my conversation with Thordis that I didn't notice him.

"What are you doing here?" he said, "Valentino, I was searching for you everywhere." It seemed that I had spent many hours talking with an imaginary person. Thordis was not there anymore.

"I apologize but I don't know what happened to me," I frankly stated to him. I started to get a bit anxious. Suddenly, I was not feeling good. My stomach began to cramp up. Felix was worried for me. Therefore, we decided to go back to the GMC Vandura van. We walked through the cemetery gates, and in short time we got into the vehicle.

After an unsuccessful day of searching, we returned at Ferdamadur Inn. Erna was sitting behind the desk, typing on a laptop. She did not pay attention to me and Felix.

I questioned myself if I had really seen Thordis at the cemetery. Felix was wondering if we should go back to Reykjavik. "Honestly speaking, I have a bad feeling about this place," he admitted, "I also perceive dark entities around us."

I agreed with Felix, but I told him to be thinking about how we could better proceed. I carefully reviewed both Jón's manuscript and my map. I looked outside and I admired a mountain towering above Skagaströnd. It is called by the locals Spákonufell.

"Erna, can you tell me what the word 'Spákonufell' means?" I inquired. She was curious about the question I asked her. "It means literally the 'Prophetess Mountain'," she promptly answered. I had the impression that she knew what I was looking for.

She was a sensitive person. Sensitive in all aspects. I had good reason to believe the Sorcerers of Hólmavík would meet somewhere on the top of that mount.

After spending a few minutes thinking about it, I made an intuitive connection between Thordis 's apparition and the sun setting behind a mountain engraved on the rock at the cemetery. Indeed, according to Icelandic sagas, Thordis the soothsayer lived at Spákonufell. She was a skilled witch.

"Valentino, you should get some extra protection. Let's see if I can find your name in this book," Erna said before we left. This sentence sounded familiar. My recurring 'Puffin Dream' was manifesting in reality.

This episode gave me one more proof that my premonitions were right.

The book she referred to, was the 'Book of Magic', called in Icelandic *Galdrabók*. It was a sixteenth century manuscript with a collection of spells and staves. She chose for me the 'Helm of Awe', a protective Viking symbol. She also offered me her precious necklace. Her elf's torc became my protective amulet.

At that point, I was truly motivated to achieve my objectives. Nevertheless, I must admit I was still worried, not knowing what to expect that evening. Nobody knew what could happen next. "Good luck Valentino. I hope you will be careful," she said. Spákonufell, the 'Prophetess Mountain', was our next destination.

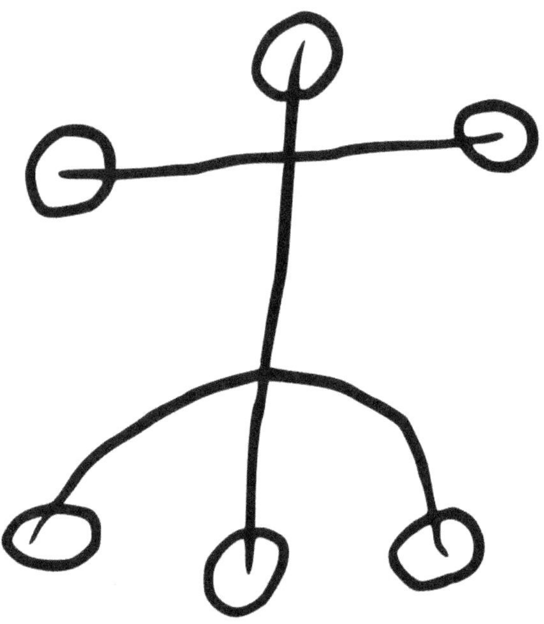

9 THE RITUAL

I examined her necklace and I thought: could I rely on it to prove the actual existence of the 'hidden people'? Was it authentic or not?

Furthermore, if the sect did exist, in some sense, Gudrun did exist too and, so, was she somewhere waiting for me? And where was she? I was starting to get disappointed in her. After all, I had come up here to meet her too.

What should I believe to be true? I wanted to believe there was a logical explanation. But I also doubted I would get a rational answer. However, Erna believed in me, and she trusted me completely. I was highly honored to carry her 'talisman'.

From the Ferdamadur Inn, I and Felix drove close to the mountain. He intended to arrive next to a walking route. This was a huge area. After only a short time, he stopped his van and we began to look around Spákonufell for clues.

We went through a narrow path. The view from up there was so strikingly beautiful. At first sight, it seemed there was no indication of any ritual setup. It would have been easy to notice someone walking up the hill.

Perhaps the adepts were hiding in a cavern. But where was the cave entrance and passageway? Or maybe they were performing the ritual somewhere else. And if so, where did they go? We decided to continue walking further.

I would say about ten minutes later a strange light appeared down our path. The road became rough, but I could see this light slowly coming towards us. It was very bright. It came up into our view and then it disappeared as if someone was carrying a lantern walking down the path.

We both started getting freaked out. Consequently, we ran back to the van. We sat there, watching this light moving closer and closer. Felix ultimately turned on the vehicle and drove back to town.

Just when everything seemed lost, help came unexpectedly. A flock of puffins showed up. They flew towards us. Again my 'Puffin Dream'. This was another sign that confirmed my premonitions.

We had the feeling that they wanted us to follow them. Felix continued to drive up to the end of a dark road, then we continued on foot. "I think the flock is taking us to the cemetery gate," I said. Indeed, we were again outside the graveyard.

Once we got there, the puffins flew away. I immediately noticed some people around a fire.

They were wearing, as expected, bird masks. They were likely the Sorcerers of Hólmavík in the act of evoking the 'hidden people'; perhaps they were even wearing Pulcinella's masks.

I could not clearly distinguish what was going on. "Valentino, let's get a closer look and hide beside a large tombstone," Felix suggested. He was a little bit concerned about the situation. Me too, but I was also excited. I was finally able to document the existence of what I had theorized earlier.

"Better they don't see us, but I would like to take photos with my smartphone," I stated. Probably, it was not a good idea. It was dark and, even though I had a great camera, I was not sure about the quality of the images.

The ritual was performed by six persons. Initially, they were concentrated on observing something. At a certain moment in the ritual, they were dancing and singing in a strange language.

My phone fell from my hand and it broke. All that noise attracted the attention of the group. One of the followers looked in our direction. Unfortunately, he saw us.

Unlike what we expected, their reaction was different. They began to panic, and then the 'self-styled Sorcerers of Hólmavík' run away from their location. Some of them took off their masks and throw them into the fire. They were nothing more than a group of Icelandic teenagers, who perhaps had simply been bored by the beginning of winter!

"Seriously? And that would be a dangerous sect with formidable occult powers?" Felix said laughing. I started to laugh as well. We approached the precise place where those guys were performing their convincing ritual. I recovered one mask from the heat. I must admit that it reminded me a lot of the Pulcinella's masks; but, notwithstanding this, it was just a masquerade ball mask.

On the surface of a stone, there was a large drawing of a chained wolf: Fenrir, I guessed. They certainly knew the Norse mythology. Apparently, the sect did not exist, or at least, if it existed, there was no trace of it in Skagaströnd graveyard.

Back at the inn, Erna was not there. I wanted to give her the necklace and tell her what the outcome was.

Probably she was already at home sleeping. I said goodnight to Felix, and I went straight to bed. We were both exhausted after an incredible day.

10 NOTHING LIKE IT SEEMS

The day after we woke up at 6:30 am. We decided to leave early and return to Reykjavik. A young lady assisted us from behind the inn's reception desk. "Doesn't Erna work today?" I asked.

"Erna? I don't know her. Only me and my brother work at Ferdamadur Inn," she replied. Rather incredibly, also Erna was a ghost or something like that. Not even Felix remembered her, and I could no longer find the talisman.

I wondered why I went through all those unexplained events, such as ghostly encounters and precognitive coincidences. For what purpose? Is it possible that it was all the result of my imagination?

We stopped only once to refuel on the way from Skagaströnd to Reykjavik. I was still tired and a little disappointed. I felt ridiculous after what had happened. Furthermore, I wondered if Felix was thinking bad about me after I had told him so many strange stories since I arrived in Iceland.

"Don't worry I believe you," he told me, seeing me that upset, "I, too, witnessed with you some unexplainable phenomena in the last days." He kept encouraging me: "Valentino, sooner or later you will do something extraordinary, something that no one has ever seen before!"

It is really true. You are most valuable to those who see and appreciate your worth. His words somehow cheered me up. Felix was undoubtedly a great friend. I could always trust him.

"Despite everything, there have been so many bizarre episodes," I continued, "My presages were real: Erna's words, the bright light, and the puffins."

I suddenly received a phone call from professor Jón. He invited me to dinner at his home in Hafnarfjörður.

"Tell your friend that he can also come tonight. He is welcomed," he gently said.

After about three hours of driving, we arrived in Suðurgata. Felix stayed in the van. He had some business to do and gave me keys to his apartment. I opened the door of his vehicle, then he quickly drove away.

I wanted to relax and sleep for a while. I went into the bedroom. I lay down on a sofa. A few moments later, I fell into a deep sleep. I don't know how long I've been resting. When I woke up completely, I saw two birds; precisely two ravens, sitting on the windowsill. They were observing me. Incredibly, they were also chatting with each other.

"I want to talk with him," Huginn said. "I don't agree. We had established that I was the spokesman today," Munnin retorted. It was just a few minutes of disagreement between the two birds, then Huginn spoke to me.

"We are Huginn and Muninn, Odin's messengers. We fly all over the world. We have been several times in Naples. It's a wonderful place. There's a person who wants to see you," Huginn stated. I was no longer surprised by those strange episodes. Deep down, they, too, were part of my premonitions from the 'Puffin Dream'.

"Would you like to follow us?" They both asked. So, I decided to go behind them out of Felix's apartment. I trusted these funny and friendly creatures. It was a cold winter day in Reykjavik. I walked for a long time, following the two birds from afar.

About one hour passed before we reached Öskjuhlíð, a hill in the center of Reykjavik. They brought me to an area covered with trees. It seemed an isolated place away from prying eyes. At one point they left me alone. I saw some people with masks coming out of the vegetation in front of me.

"Hello Valentino. You were looking for us. Here we are," one adept said to me. They were the original Sorcerers of Hólmavík. I was totally stunned, confused and scared. What did they want from me?

"Nothing is as it seems, and the truth is not what you think of us," another follower affirmed, touching my left hand.

They considered themselves the guardians of humanity. In fact, the sect was an ancient secret society formed by extraordinary men from all over the world. It had formed in the past and still existed today. The druids met every winter solstice in a secret location. They revealed to me that demons are everywhere. "We are not always able to save lives. Evil spirits are dangerous and fierce. They hate human beings," a woman's voice said. Therefore, they prevented through their 'puffin ritual' further catastrophes on the earth.

"Remember Valentino, each person has a twin soul which is supposed to be his other half. This is the reason why you desired so much to meet Gudrun again," the woman's voice uttered.

It was sad to admit it, but Gudrun was not real and not even a ghost. She was my ideal woman. The right companion. A Platonic love that does not exist and cannot disappoint either. Definitely a purely spiritual love, that created a relationship with no fear, as she was never with me in the first place. Consequently, it didn't create any expectations.

"Now it's time to wake up," somebody whispered to me. The alarm clock sounded. I was not at Felix's house. I was not in Reykjavik. I was not even in Skagaströnd. I was not in Iceland anymore. I found myself awakened in the bed of my room in Naples. It was an imaginary experience. My father knocked at the door. "Valentino, get ready, then I'll take you to the airport," he said.

Apparently, I hadn't left yet. I didn't meet Gudrun in the streets of my city. I didn't talk to Carlo Cacciatori on the plane. I didn't re-embrace my friend Felix Ortega. Jón and Fanney didn't speak to me about the hidden people. I didn't receive from Erna her protective amulet. Thordis didn't foretell my future at the cemetery. Huginn and Muninn didn't accompany me to the Sorcerers of Hólmavík.

The reality was different from my expectations. Was that reality even real? Sometimes I had the feeling of confusing reality with imagination; as if this world was connected to another. I wonder if this was my suggestion, or there was a parallel world. Perhaps, the two dimensions were somewhat interconnected.

Let's put it in this way: our reality could be defined as a kind of radio station in the middle of a plurality of other stations and frequencies.

Sometimes there would be interference between these different dimensions. It could be at this precise moment that unexplained phenomena would arise. Is this possible?

Despite everything, I learned so much on that fantasy journey, which helped me to overcome my fears and understand myself better. I am certain this dream was a way for my soul to communicate something to me.

Perhaps, it was my subconscious telling where I was in life. Our subconscious and our soul are strongly connected to each other: therefore, it's possible that they both act as a guide.

I was my own worst enemy as I doubted myself almost on everything. This weird experience enabled me to see beyond appearances.

Like my grandmother Giuseppina used to say, once you see beyond appearances, you can love everyone and have everyone love you. This woman inspired me as a child. She introduced me to literature and the love of reading in general. I realized how much she influenced my worldview. And I thank her profusely.

That morning I was rising like a phoenix from my ashes. I was in a state of consciousness that allowed me to see both the outside world and my inner spirit. In other words, I became an observer of myself and others, but I learned to watch without making any judgment.

I am now more aware that life is understanding, acceptance, and loyalty. We are meant to be grateful for who and what we have. There are unexpected opportunities in the lives of all of us, that can occur only when we are free from cultural barriers, mental superstructures, and stereotypes.

Heraclitus of Ephesus, an ancient Greek philosopher, once said that "there is nothing permanent except change." We need to reinvent ourselves repeatedly because nothing in life is constant.

This transformation allowed me to be myself and do what I always wanted to do. I love the concept of understanding yourself. I was able to expand my horizon before and after an incredible journey.

ABOUT THE AUTHOR

Valerio Gargiulo is an Italian writer of supernatural fiction and fantasy. Gargiulo was born September 26, 1979, in Naples, Italy. He has been active both in the field of legal advice and research. He studied at Reykjavik University and finished his Master of Laws in 2015. Previously, after completing a Bachelor of Laws at University of Naples Federico II, he has been freelancing, drafting reports and legal agreements. He also worked as a preschool teacher and EEG technologist.

www.ingramcontent.com/pod-product-compliance
Lightning Source LLC
Chambersburg PA
CBHW050536160726
48003CB00002B/625